WILD ACTION NEWS
CHEETAH CHASES THE STORY
by J.L. Anderson

illustrated by Amanda Erb

D1308277

Rourke
Educational Media

A Division of
Carson
Dellosa
Education®

rourkeeducationalmedia.com

Dear Guardian/Educator,
Introduce your child to the wonderful world of reading with our leveled
readers. Your growing reader will be continuously engaged as he or she
is guided from one level to the next. Each level is carefully built to provide
your child with the reading skills and knowledge to be a confident
reader! Ultimately, we want your child to develop a love of reading.

Level 1 *Learning to Read*
High frequency words, basic sentences, large type, labels, full color
illustrations to help young readers better comprehend the text

Level 2 *Beginning to Read Alone*
Short sentences, familiar words, simple plot, easy-to-read fonts

Level 3 *Reading on Your Own*
Short paragraphs, easy-to-follow plots, vocabulary is increasingly
challenging, exciting stories

Level 4 *Proficient Reader*
Chapters, engaging stories, challenging vocabulary, multiple text features

Reading should be a pleasurable experience. A child who enjoys reading
reads more, and a child who reads more becomes a better reader.
Your child will grow with exposure to broad vocabulary and literary
techniques, and will develop deeper critical thinking and comprehension
skills. We are excited to be a part of your child's reading journey.

Happy reading,
Rourke Educational Media

© 2020 Rourke Educational Media

All rights reserved. No part of this book may be
reproduced or utilized in any form or by any means,
electronic or mechanical including photocopying,
recording, or by any information storage and
retrieval system without permission in writing from
the publisher.

www.rourkeeducationalmedia.com

Edited by: Kim Thompson
Cover and interior layout by: Rhea Magaro-Wallace
Cover and interior illustrations by: Amanda Erb

Library of Congress PCN Data

Cheetah Chases the Story / J.L. Anderson
(WILD Action News)
ISBN 978-1-73161-501-5 (hard cover)(alk. paper)
ISBN 978-1-73161-308-0 (soft cover)
ISBN 978-1-73161-606-7 (e-Book)
ISBN 978-1-73161-711-8 (e-Pub)
Library of Congress Control Number: 2019932317

Printed in the United States of America,
North Mankato, Minnesota

Table of Contents

Chapter One
Savanna Secrets

Life on our wildlife preserve on the savanna is fast-paced. I like a fast pace. I'm Cheetah! My body is made for speed.

My legs are long. My body is slender. I can run faster than any other animal!

But this isn't about how
great I am. I am meeting
Warthog on business.

Don't worry. The business
is not eating Warthog. I am a
predator. But I try not to eat
my sources.

I am a WILD Action News reporter. Warthog has a news **tip**. That makes him a news source!

"Some animals are leaving

the preserve," Warthog says.

We are safe on the preserve.

Humans cannot hunt here.

Why would animals leave our safe home? *Sniff, sniff.* I smell a story. I need to get the **scoop**!

"Why are they leaving?" I ask. "Where are they going?"

Reporters ask questions to gather facts. They share the facts with others. Reporters keep everyone informed!

Chapter Two

Dangerous Information

"Hyena saw something,"
Warthog says. "I heard her
laughing about it."

Oh, no. I don't like hyenas.
One tried to eat me when
I was a cub. Hyenas think
cheetah cubs are a tasty treat.

Still, I have a job to do. If Hyena saw something, I must **interview** her.

I thank Warthog. Time to search for Hyena!

I do not have much time.

I have a **deadline** to meet.

Good thing I am a fast runner.

I can sprint as fast as a car!

My eyesight is super too.

I can see three miles away!

I stop when I see Hyena.

I am thirsty from my run. I do not see any water to drink. The savanna has been dry lately.

"It's the cute little reporter,"
Hyena says. She licks her
paws. "You are lucky I just ate."
Gulp. I do not want to be a
snack. But I need the facts.

I put on my bravest face.

"Do you know why animals
are leaving the preserve?"
I ask.

Hyena laughs. She walks in
a slow circle around me.
I watch her closely. I am fast,
but I am not a fighter.

"The lions are planning a party," she says. "They will not invite me. But I will still go. I will eat all their food!" she laughs.

Chapter Three
Hunting for the Story

A party? Is this true? I don't know if Hyena is a **credible** news source. I'll have to find out myself.

"Thanks!" I say. I get out of there fast.

I search the preserve. I spot
a pride of lions.

"Is the little reporter here for
a roaring contest?" Lion asks.

The lions laugh.

Cheetahs cannot roar like other big cats. But we can bark!

"I will bark all day for answers!" I say. "Are you planning a party?"

"No," Lion says. "But a
party sounds fun!"

The other lions agree.

"Let's plan a party!"

"Will you leave the
preserve?" I ask.

"No," Lion says. "It is
too dangerous."

I take notes on the party plans. That's a story for another day!

A herd of wildebeests runs by.

"What's going on?" I call to them.

"I'm following the herd,"

Wildebeest says.

"Goodbye, lions!" I say.

I follow the herd too.

The wildebeests run and
run. But I stop. I see my scoop!
I see elephants digging a
hole. A big hole! The hole is
filled with water.

Many animals drink from the hole.

"Do you know it is not safe here?" I ask. "We are outside the preserve."

"We are so thirsty," the animals say.

"There are safer places to dig," I say.

We move back inside the preserve. The elephants dig again. The other animals help.

This news story will help keep the animal community safe!

Bonus Stuff!

Glossary

credible (KRED-uh-buhl): Believable.

deadline (DED-line): A time when something must be completed.

interview (IN-tur-vyoo): To ask questions in order to gather information.

scoop (skoop): A story reported by a news organization before other news organizations have reported it.

tip (tip): Helpful information.

Discussion Questions

1. Why does Cheetah talk to Hyena even though she doesn't want to?

2. When she writes her news story, do you think Cheetah will include information about the lions' party? Why or why not?

3. How will it help the animals on the savanna to read the information in Cheetah's news story?

Activity: Speed Game

How fast is a cheetah? A warthog? A person running? A car? Learn about the speeds of moving things. Make a game to play with a friend.

Supplies

- computer with internet and printer
- scissors
- three sheets of heavy paper
- glue or tape
- black marker

Directions

1. With an adult, do internet research to find out the speeds of 18 things. They can be animals, people in motion, or vehicles. Print and cut out a small picture of each thing.
2. Cut each sheet of paper into six rectangles to make 18 playing cards.
3. Tape or glue a picture on each card.
4. Write a speed on the back of each card. For example, on the back of the cheetah card, write 70 miles per hour (113 kilometers per hour) because cheetahs can run about that fast.
5. Deal the cards to you and a friend. On each turn, play a card. The card with the faster speed takes the hand. Keep playing until the winner has all the cards.

Writing Prompt

Cheetah reported about a change in her community: The search for water was leading some animals outside the safety of the preserve. What is changing around you? It could be something happening in your home, school, neighborhood, or city. Write a news story about it. Be sure to answer *what, where, when, who, why,* and *how.*

About the Author

J.L. Anderson is always curious to get the scoop! She loves writing for kids of all ages, and she's passionate about animals and nature. You can learn more about her by visiting www.jessicaleeanderson.com.

About the Illustrator

Amanda is always on the lookout for new stories to illustrate! Some of her favorite stories to illustrate involve expressive animal and human characters. You can find more of her work at www.amandaerb.com.